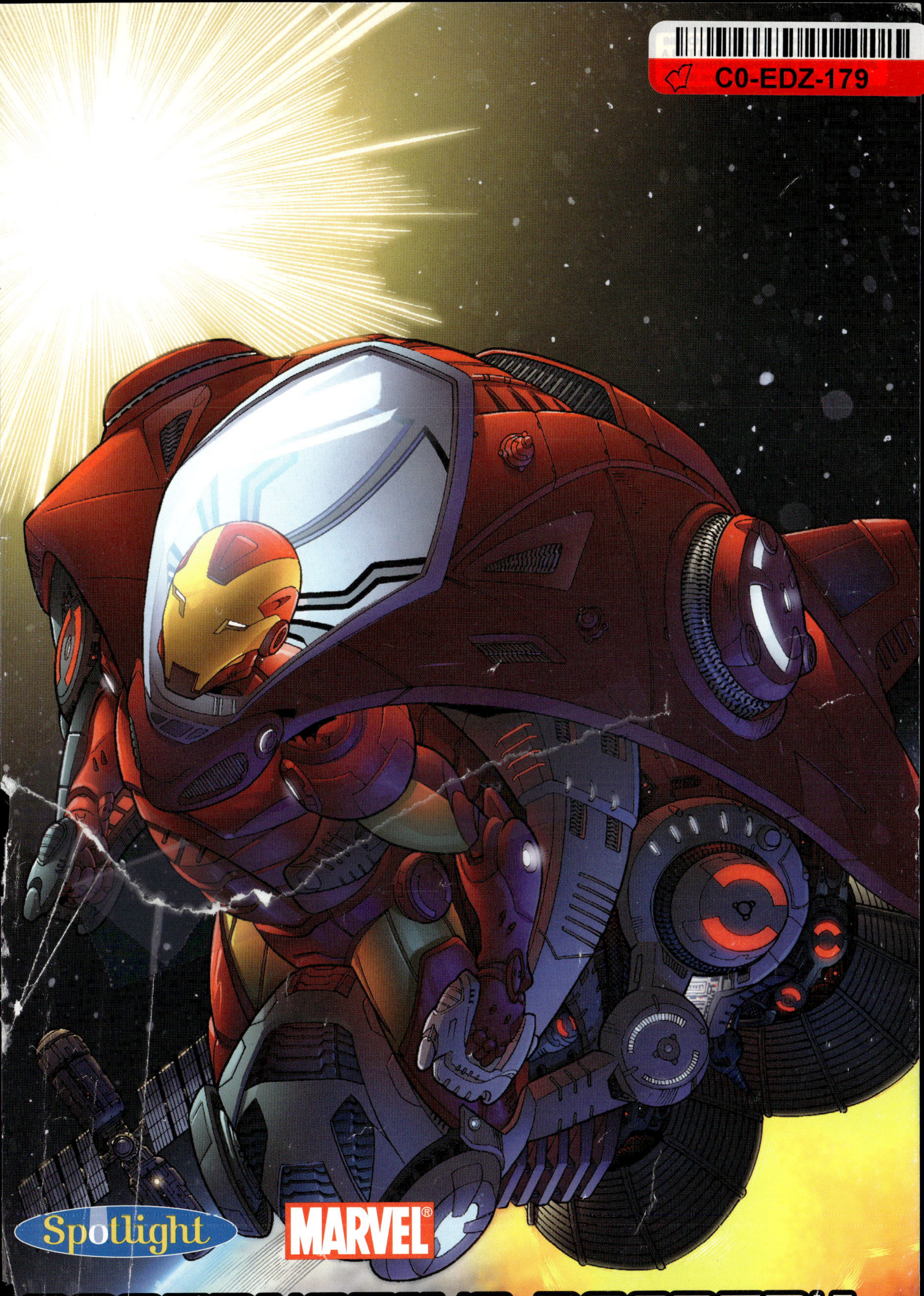

Spotlight MARVEL

DESTRUCTIVE REENTRY

FRED VAN LENTE WRITER
JAMES CORDEIRO PENCILER
GARY ERSKINE INKER
MARTEGOD GRACIA COLORIST
DAVE SHARPE LETTERER
SKOTTIE YOUNG COVER
ANTHONY DIAL PRODUCTION
NATHAN COSBY ASST. EDITOR
MARK PANICCIA EDITOR
JOE QUESADA EDITOR IN CHIEF
DAN BUCKLEY PUBLISHER

VISIT US AT
www.abdopublishing.com

Reinforced library bound edition published in 2009 by Spotlight, a division of the ABDO Group, 8000 West 78th Street, Edina, Minnesota 55439. Spotlight produces high-quality reinforced library bound editions for schools and libraries. Published by agreement with Marvel Characters, Inc.

MARVEL, and all related character names and the distinctive likenesses thereof are trademarks of Marvel Characters, Inc., and is/are used with permission. Copyright © 2009 Marvel Characters, Inc. All rights reserved. www.marvel.com

MARVEL, Iron Man: TM & © 2009 Marvel Characters, Inc. All rights reserved. www.marvel.com. This book is produced under license from Marvel Characters, Inc.

Library of Congress Cataloging-in-Publication Data

Van Lente, Fred.
  Destructive reentry / Fred Van Lente, writer ; James Cordeiro, penciler ; Gary Erskine, inker ; Martegod Gracia, colorist ; Dave Sharpe, letterer ; Skottie Young, cover. -- Reinforced library bound ed.
     p. cm. -- (Iron Man)
  "Marvel."
  ISBN 978-1-59961-589-9
  1. Graphic novels. [1. Graphic novels. 2. Superheroes--Fiction.] I. Cordeiro, James, ill. II. Title.
  PZ7.7.V26De 2009
  741.5'973--dc22
                                                        2008033395

All Spotlight books have reinforced library bindings and are manufactured in the United States of America.

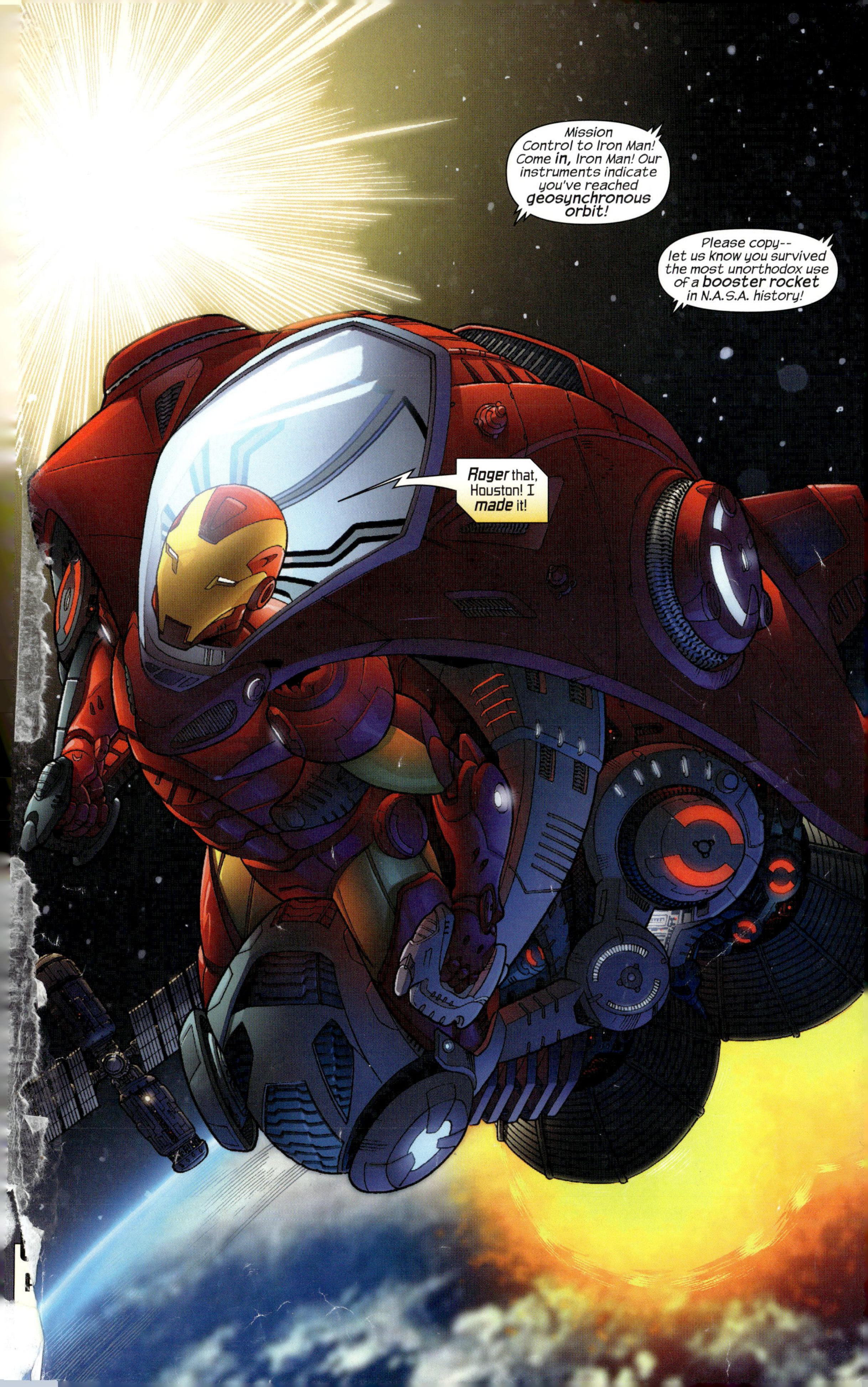
Mission Control to Iron Man! Come in, Iron Man! Our instruments indicate you've reached geosynchronous orbit!
Please copy-- let us know you survived the most unorthodox use of a booster rocket in N.A.S.A. history!
Roger that, Houston! I made it!

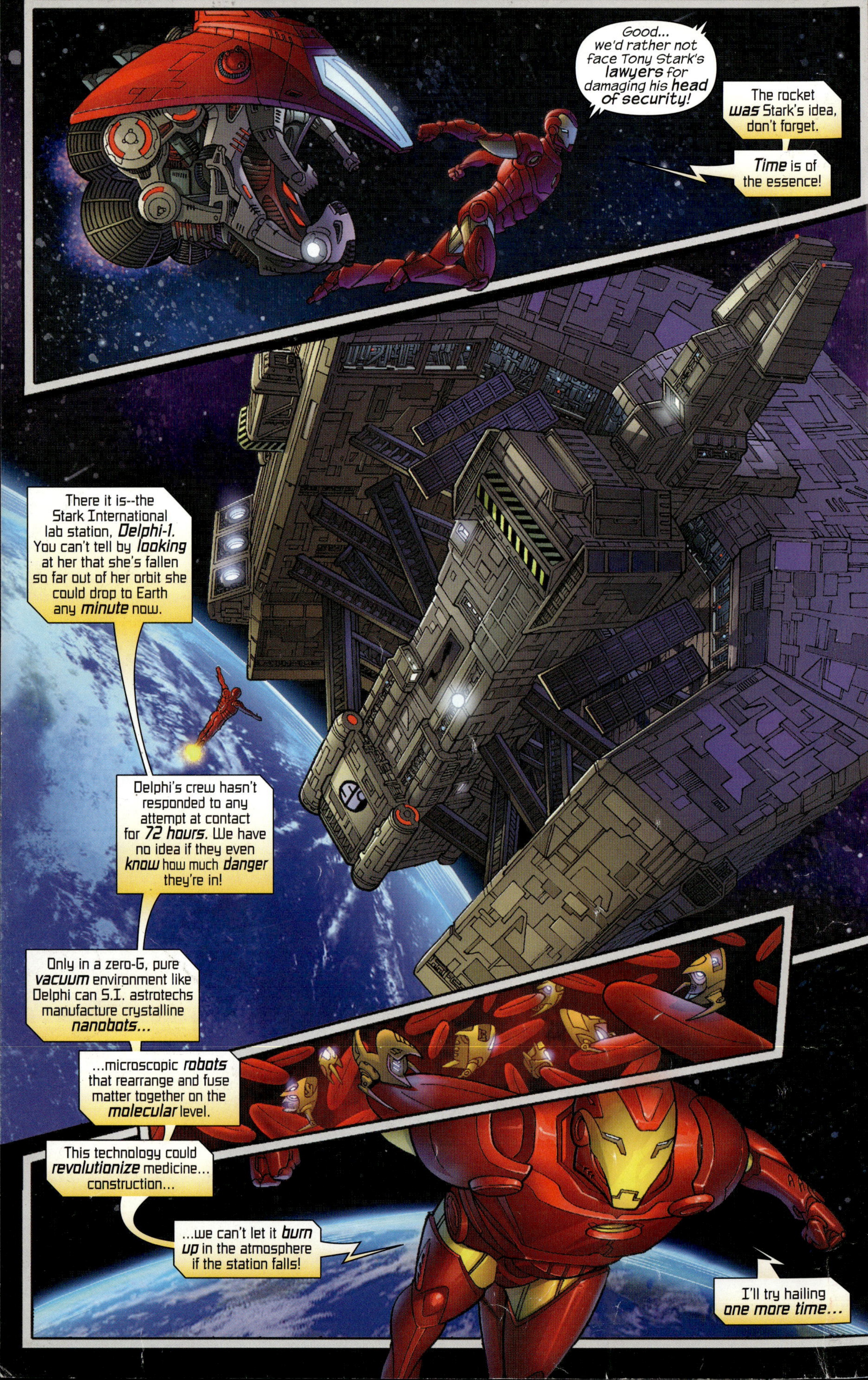

Good... we'd rather not face Tony Stark's lawyers for damaging his head of security!
The rocket was Stark's idea, don't forget.
Time is of the essence!
There it is--the Stark International lab station, Delphi-1. You can't tell by looking at her that she's fallen so far out of her orbit she could drop to Earth any minute now.
Delphi's crew hasn't responded to any attempt at contact for 72 hours. We have no idea if they even know how much danger they're in!
Only in a zero-G, pure vacuum environment like Delphi can S.I. astrotechs manufacture crystalline nanobots...
...microscopic robots that rearrange and fuse matter together on the molecular level.
This technology could revolutionize medicine... construction...
...we can't let it burn up in the atmosphere if the station falls!
I'll try hailing one more time...

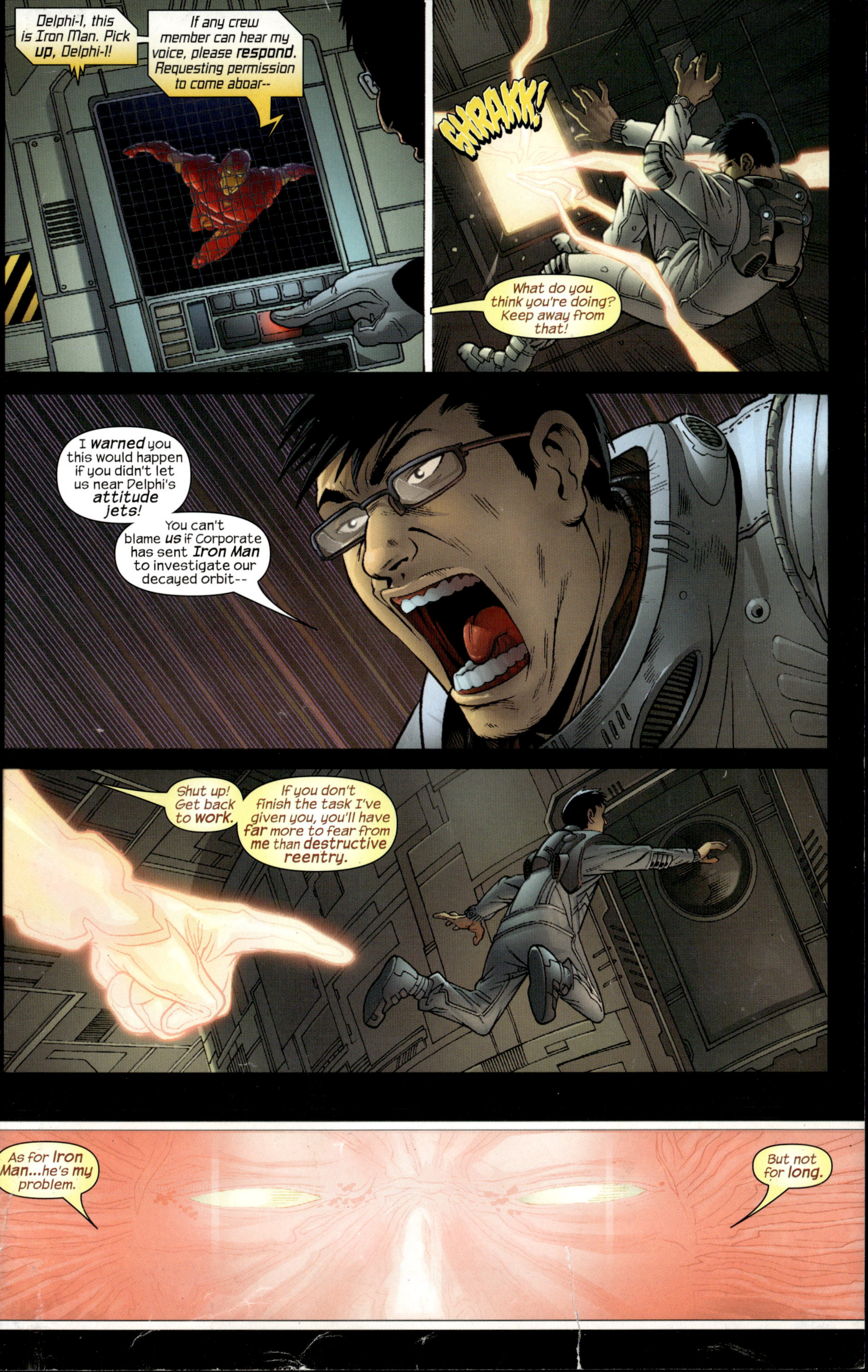
Delphi-1, this is Iron Man. Pick up, Delphi-1!
If any crew member can hear my voice, please respond. Requesting permission to come aboar--
SHRAKK!
What do you think you're doing? Keep away from that!
I warned you this would happen if you didn't let us near Delphi's attitude jets!
You can't blame us if Corporate has sent Iron Man to investigate our decayed orbit--
Shut up! Get back to work.
If you don't finish the task I've given you, you'll have far more to fear from me than destructive reentry.
As for Iron Man...he's my problem.
But not for long.

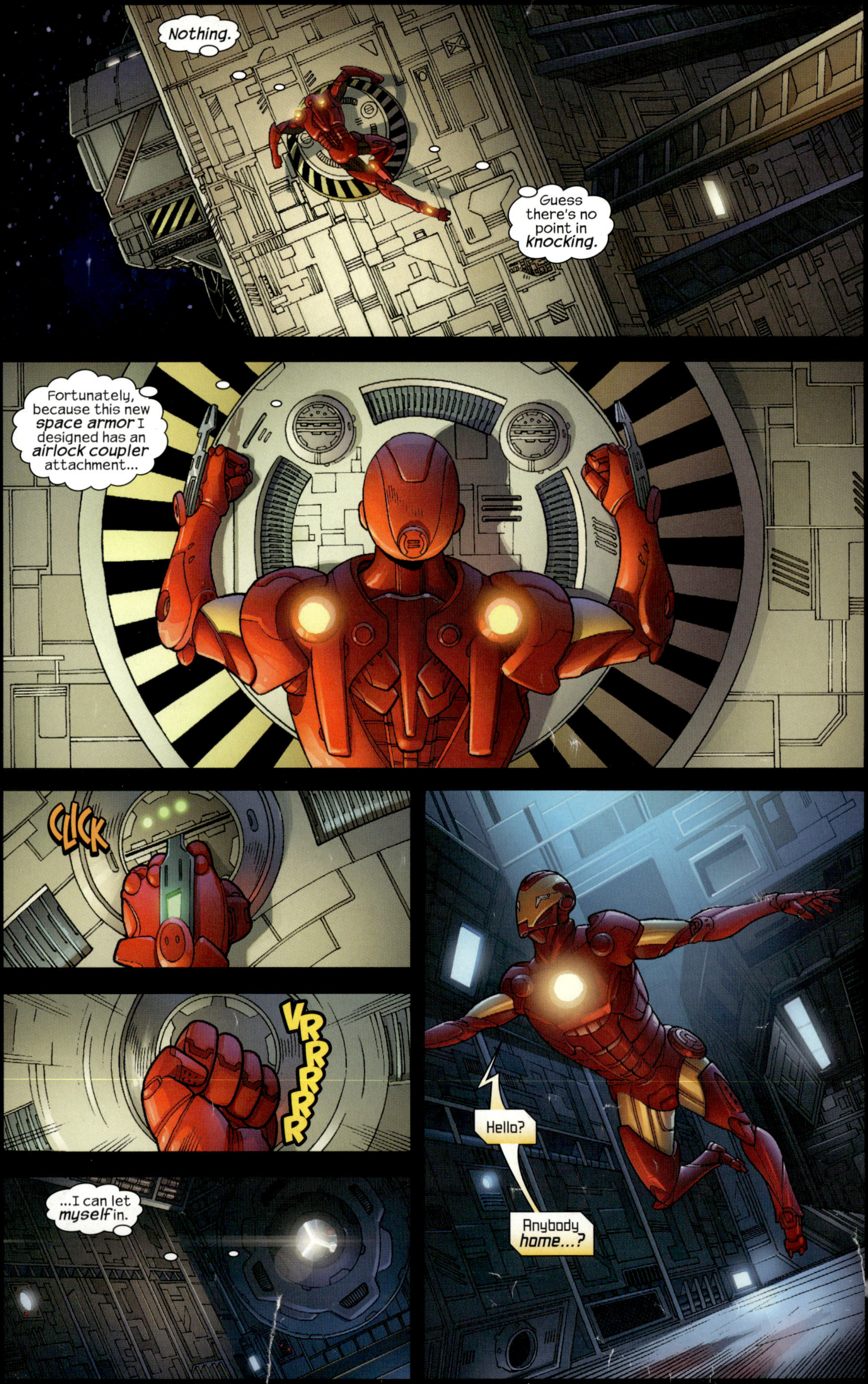

Nothing.
Guess there's no point in knocking.
Fortunately, because this new space armor I designed has an airlock coupler attachment...
CLICK
VRRRRR
...I can let myself in.
Hello?
Anybody home...?

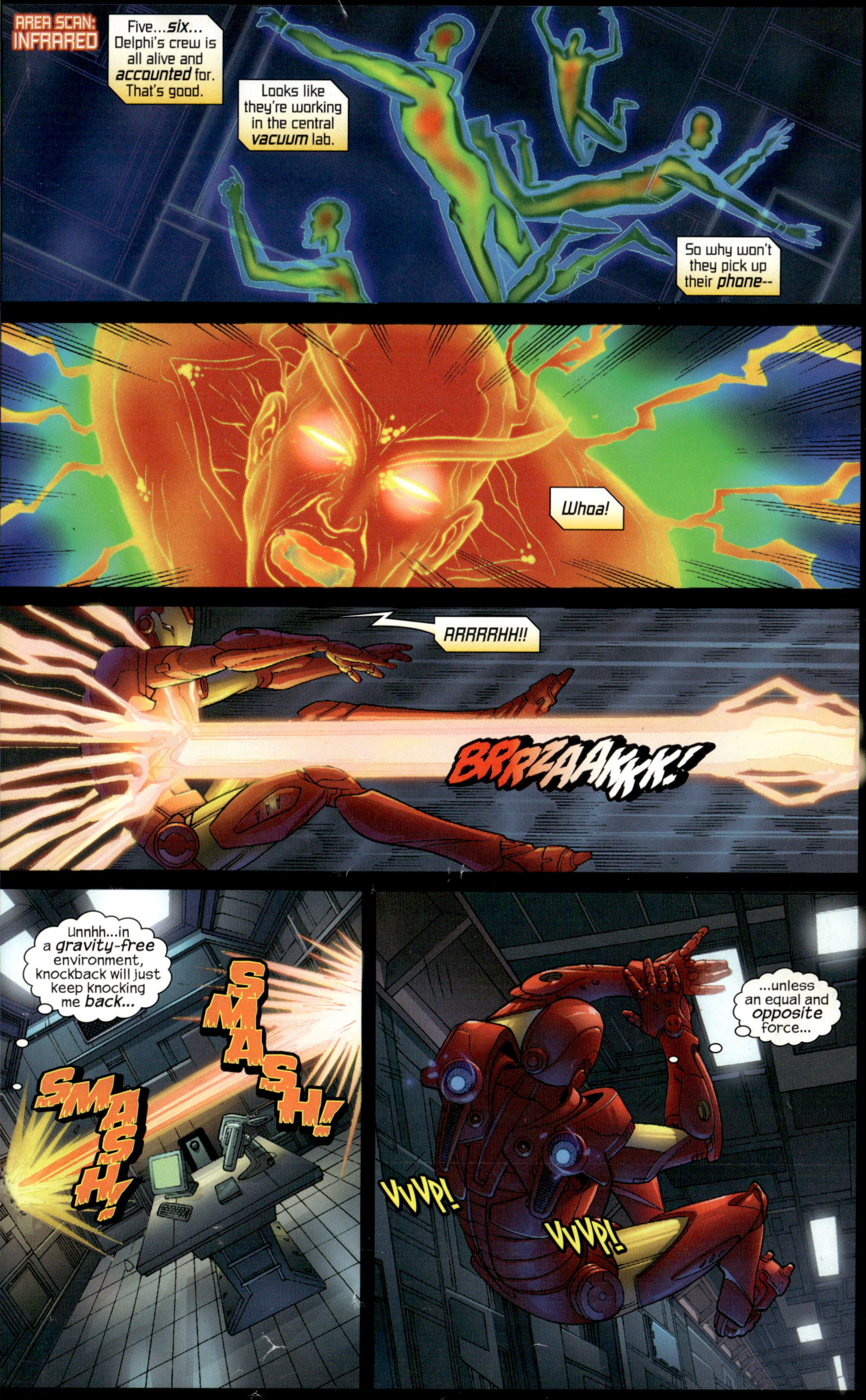
AREA SCAN: INFRARED
Five...six... Delphi's crew is all alive and accounted for. That's good.
Looks like they're working in the central vacuum lab.
So why won't they pick up their phone--
Whoa!
ARRRRHH!!
BRRZAAKKK!
Unnhh...in a gravity-free environment, knockback will just keep knocking me back...
SMASH!
SMASH!
...unless an equal and opposite force...
VVVP!
VVVP!

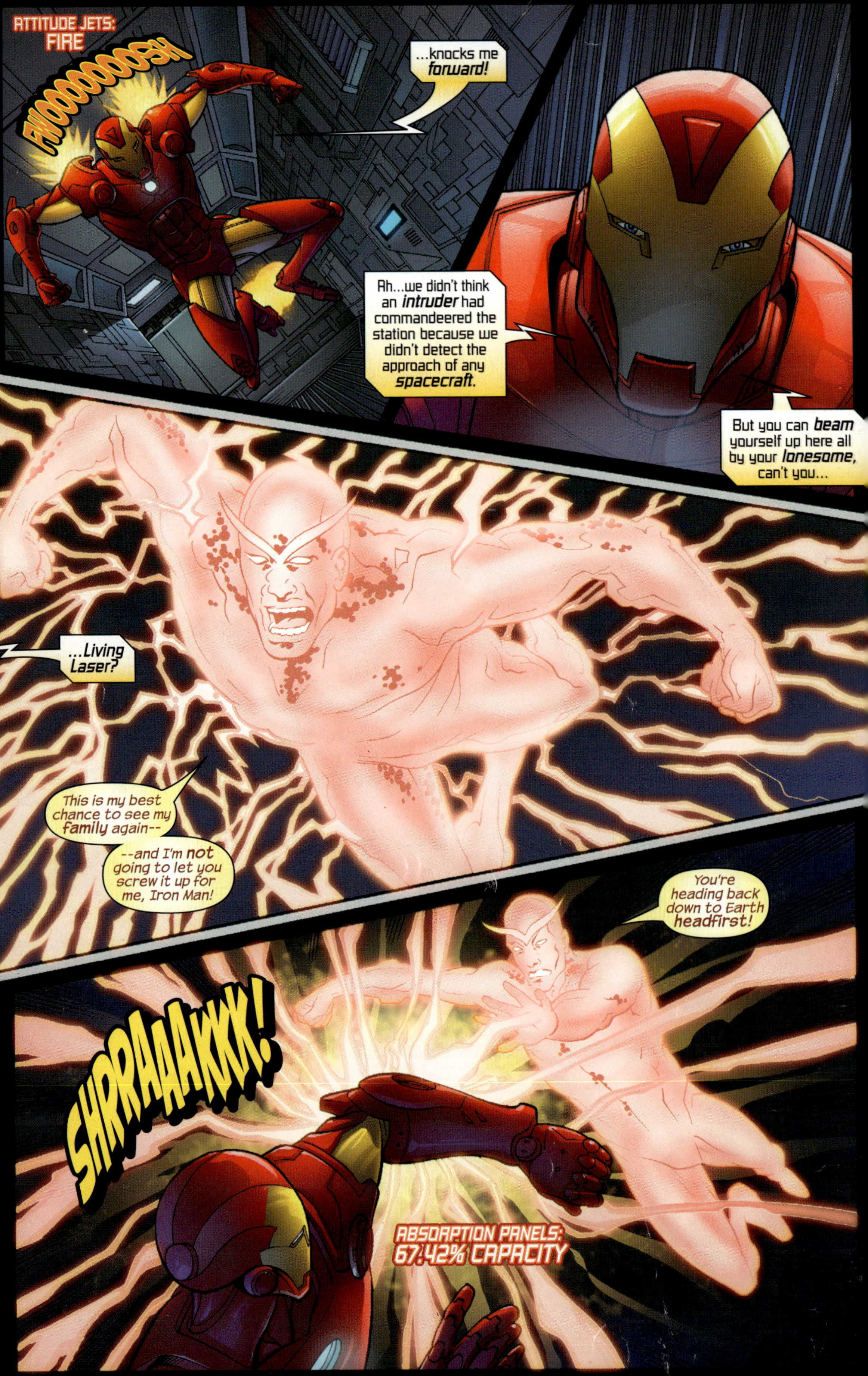
ATTITUDE JETS: FIRE
FWOOOOOOSH
...knocks me forward!
Ah...we didn't think an intruder had commandeered the station because we didn't detect the approach of any spacecraft.
But you can beam yourself up here all by your lonesome, can't you...
...Living Laser?
This is my best chance to see my family again--
--and I'm not going to let you screw it up for me, Iron Man!
You're heading back down to Earth headfirst!
SHRRAAAKKK!
ABSORPTION PANELS: 67.42% CAPACITY

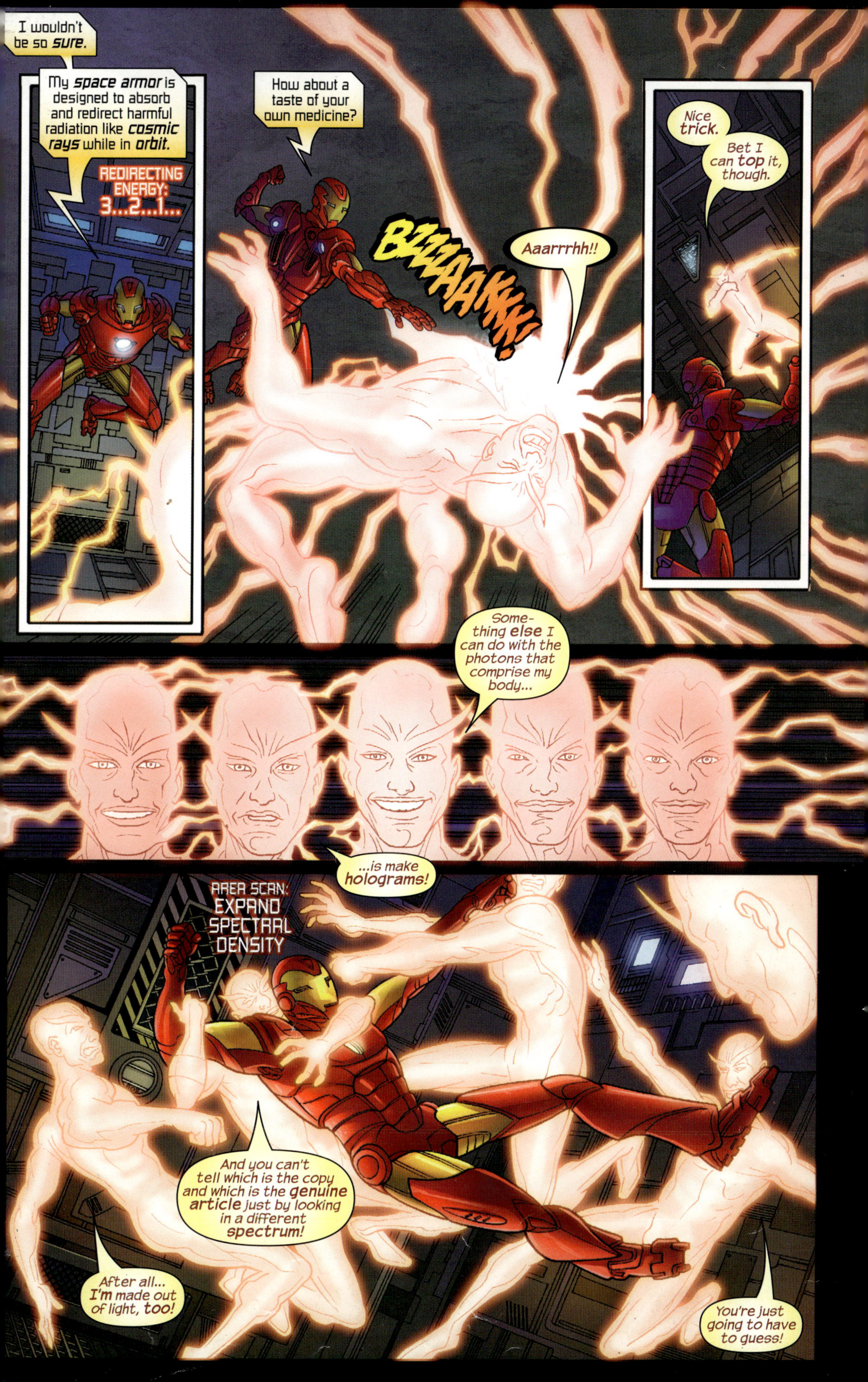
I wouldn't be so sure.
My space armor is designed to absorb and redirect harmful radiation like cosmic rays while in orbit.
REDIRECTING ENERGY: 3...2...1...
How about a taste of your own medicine?
BZZAAKKK!
Aaarrrhh!!
Nice trick.
Bet I can top it, though.
Some-thing else I can do with the photons that comprise my body...
...is make holograms!
AREA SCAN: EXPAND SPECTRAL DENSITY
And you can't tell which is the copy and which is the genuine article just by looking in a different spectrum!
After all... I'm made out of light, too!
You're just going to have to guess!

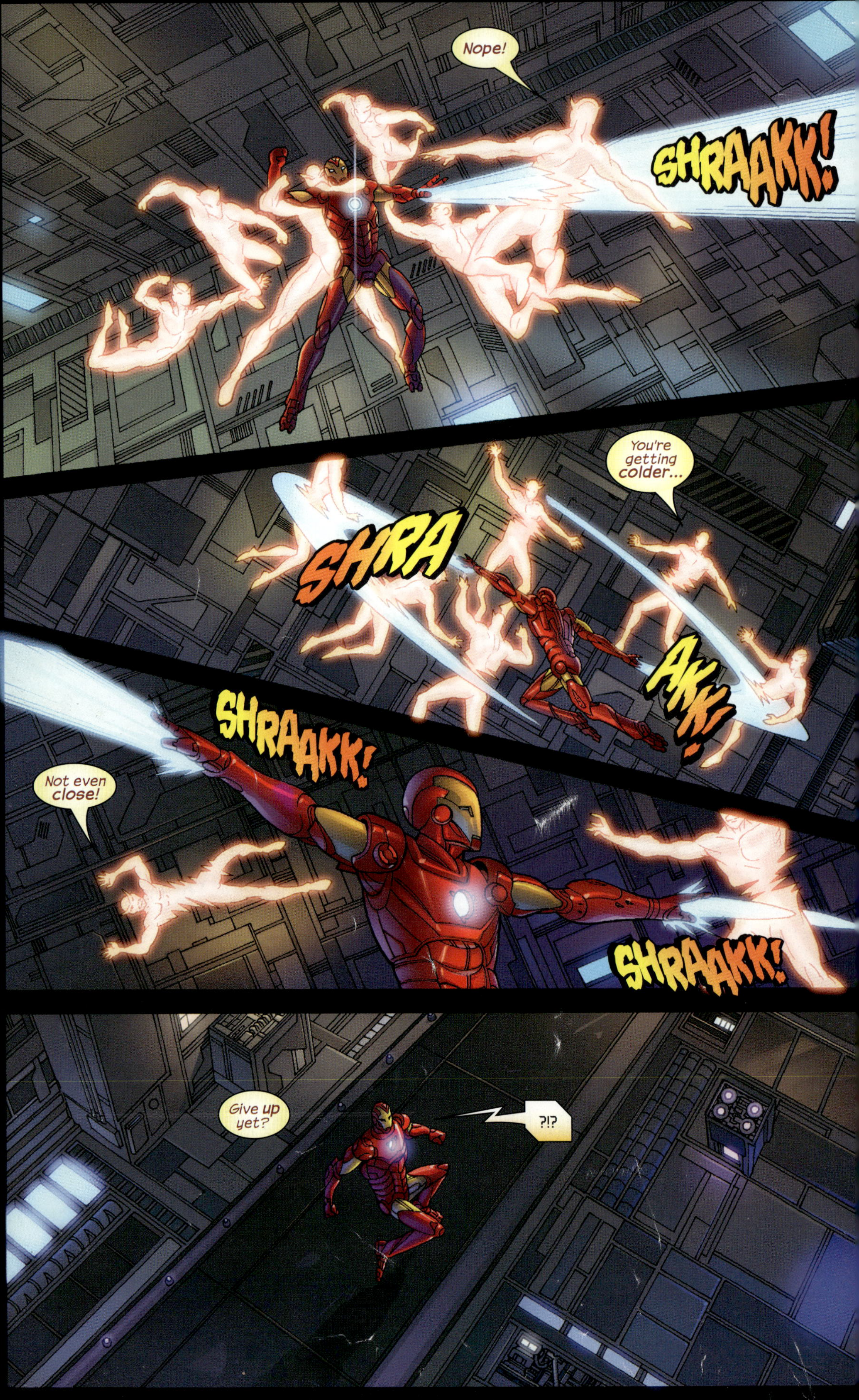
Nope!
SHRAAKK!
You're getting colder...
SHRA
AKK!
SHRAAKK!
Not even close!
SHRAAKK!
Give up yet?
?!?

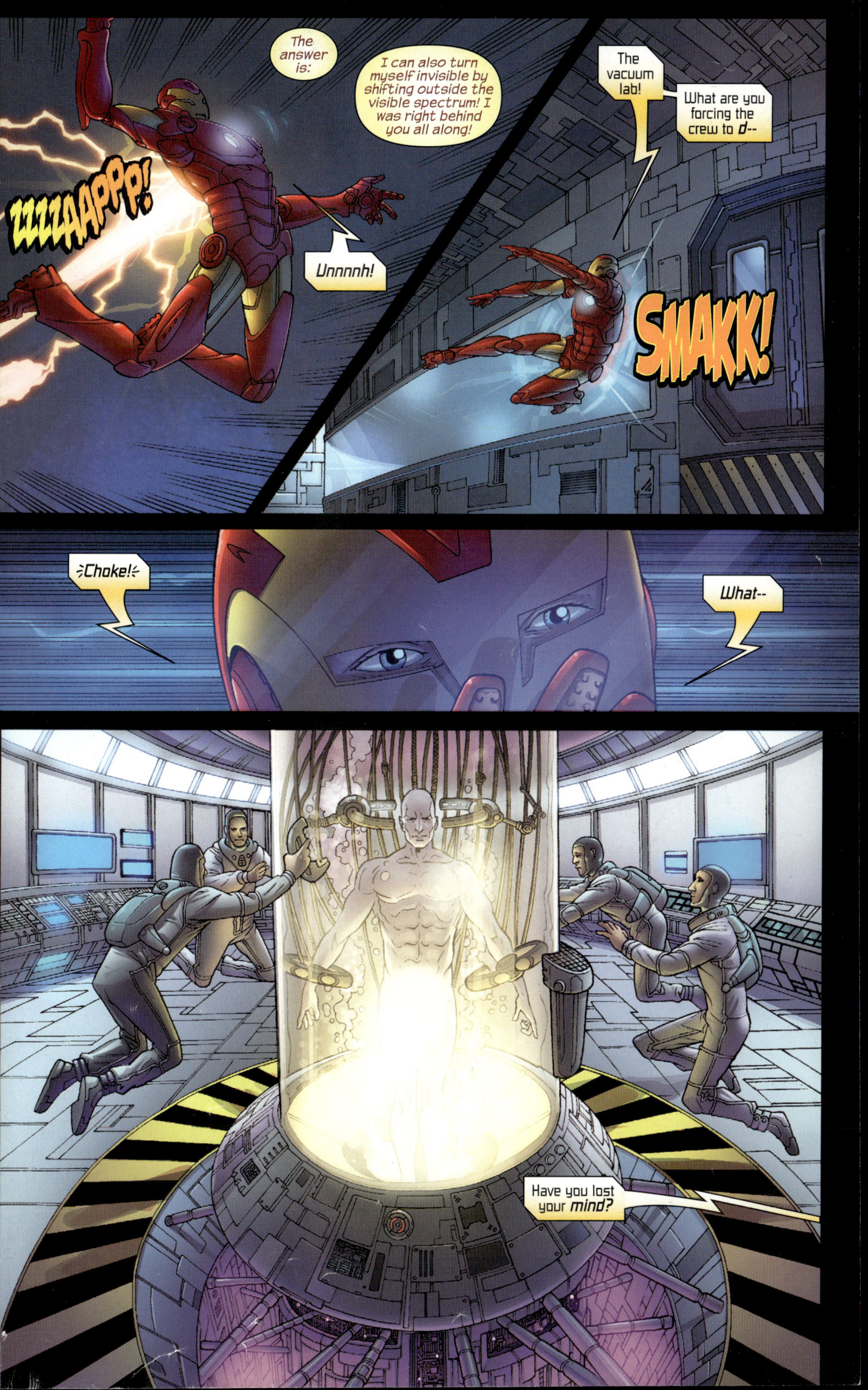
The answer is:
I can also turn myself invisible by shifting outside the visible spectrum! I was right behind you all along!
ZZZZAAPPP!
Unnnnh!
The vacuum lab!
What are you forcing the crew to d--
SMAKK!
Choke!
What--
Have you lost your *mind?*

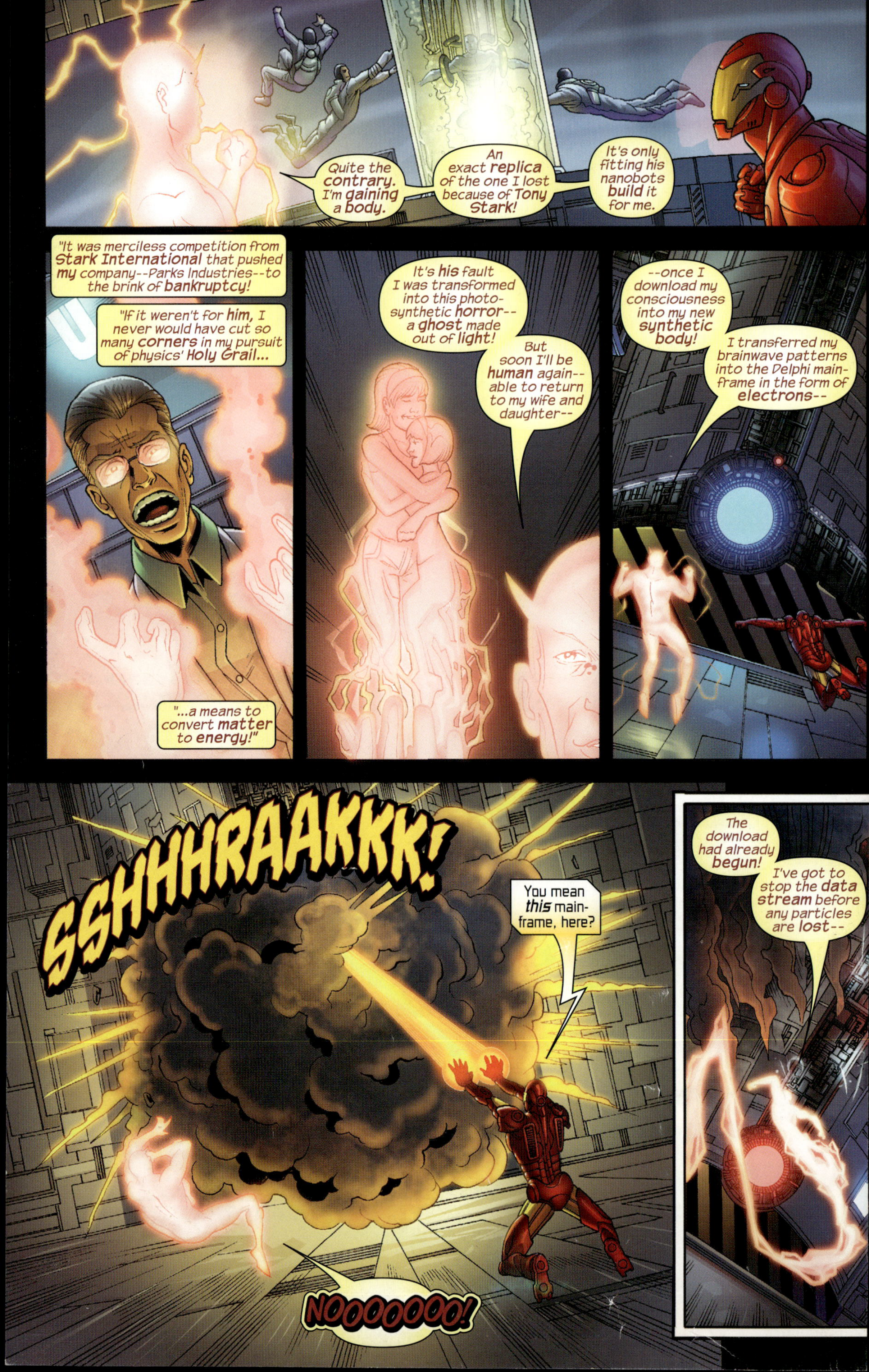
Quite the contrary. I'm gaining a body.
An exact replica of the one I lost because of Tony Stark!
It's only fitting his nanobots build it for me.
"It was merciless competition from Stark International that pushed my company--Parks Industries--to the brink of bankruptcy!
"If it weren't for him, I never would have cut so many corners in my pursuit of physics' Holy Grail...
"...a means to convert matter to energy!"
It's his fault I was transformed into this photo-synthetic horror--a ghost made out of light!
But soon I'll be human again--able to return to my wife and daughter--
--once I download my consciousness into my new synthetic body!
I transferred my brainwave patterns into the Delphi main-frame in the form of electrons--
SSHHHRAAKKK!
You mean this main-frame, here?
NOOOOOOO!
The download had already begun!
I've got to stop the data stream before any particles are lost--

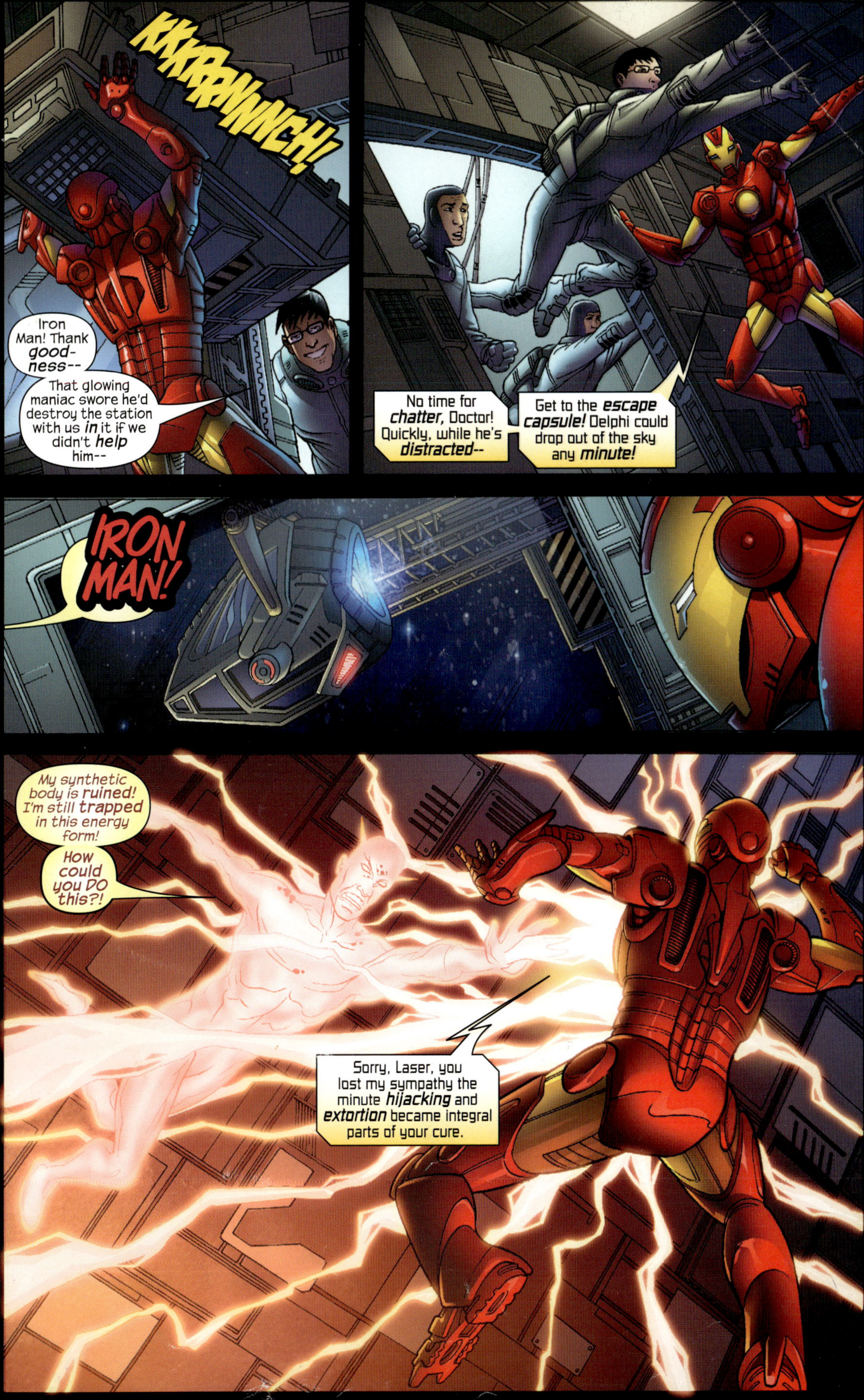

KKKRNNNCH!
Iron Man! Thank good-ness--
That glowing maniac swore he'd destroy the station with us in it if we didn't help him--
No time for chatter, Doctor! Quickly, while he's distracted--
Get to the escape capsule! Delphi could drop out of the sky any minute!
IRON MAN!
My synthetic body is ruined! I'm still trapped in this energy form!
How could you DO this?!
Sorry, Laser, you lost my sympathy the minute hijacking and extortion became integral parts of your cure.

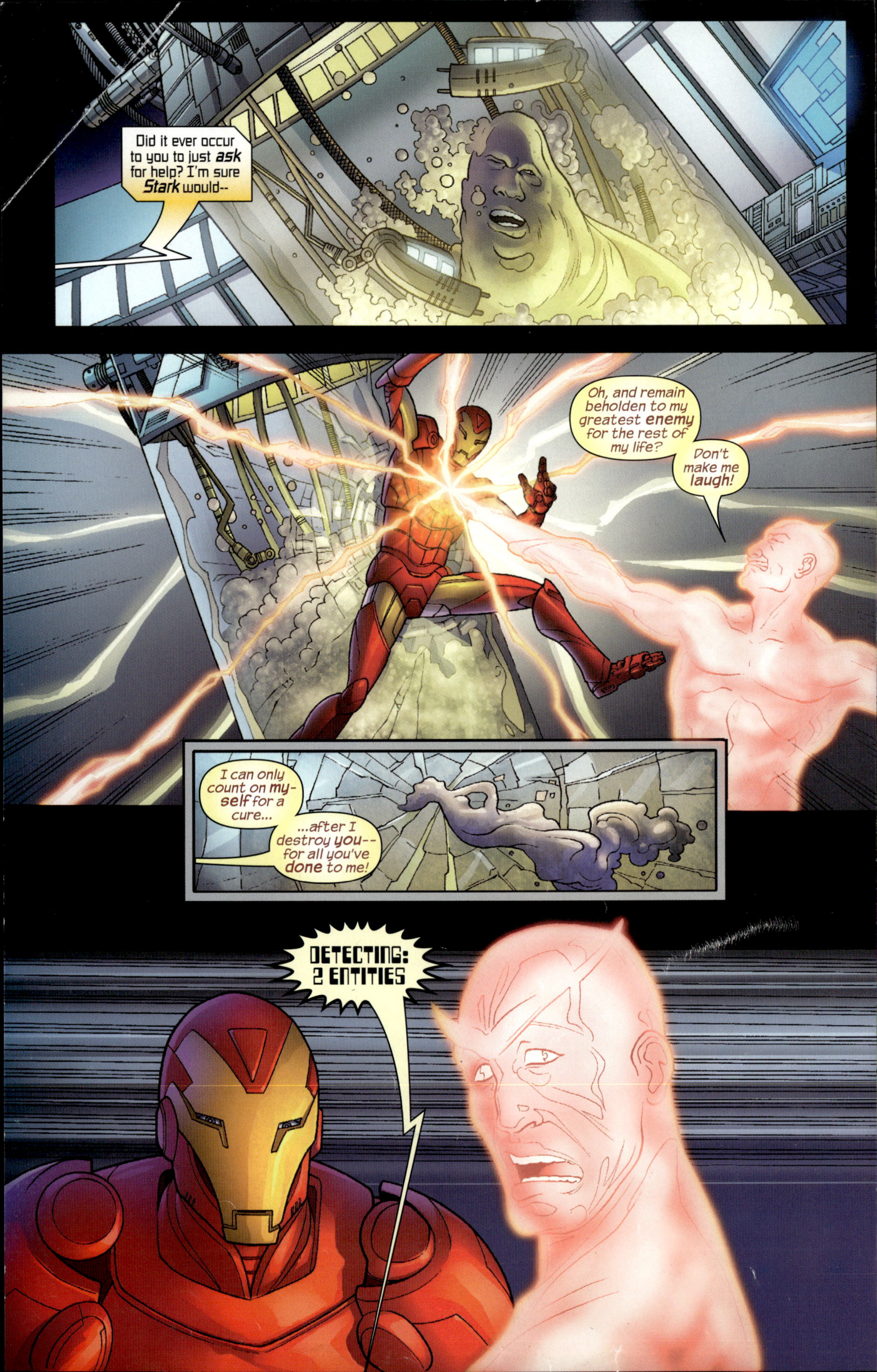

Did it ever occur to you to just *ask* for help? I'm sure *Stark* would--
Oh, and remain beholden to my greatest **enemy** for the rest of my life?
Don't make me **laugh!**
I can only count on **my-self** for a cure...
...after I destroy **you**-- for all you've **done** to me!
DETECTING: 2 ENTITIES

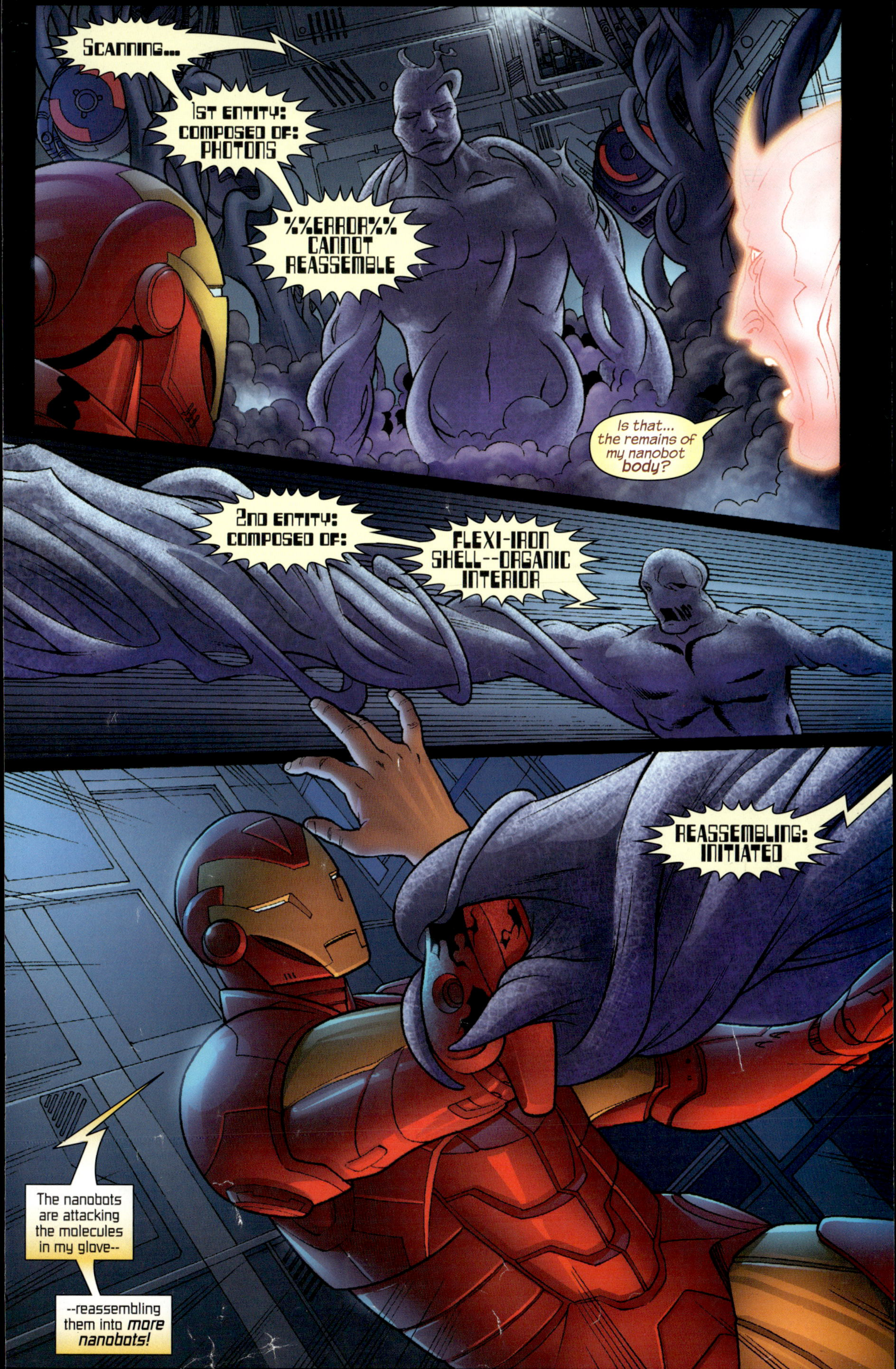
Scanning...
1st Entity: Composed of: Photons
%%Error%% Cannot Reassemble
Is that... the remains of my nanobot body?
2nd Entity: Composed of:
Flexi-Iron Shell--Organic Interior
Reassembling: Initiated
The nanobots are attacking the molecules in my glove--
--reassembling them into more nanobots!

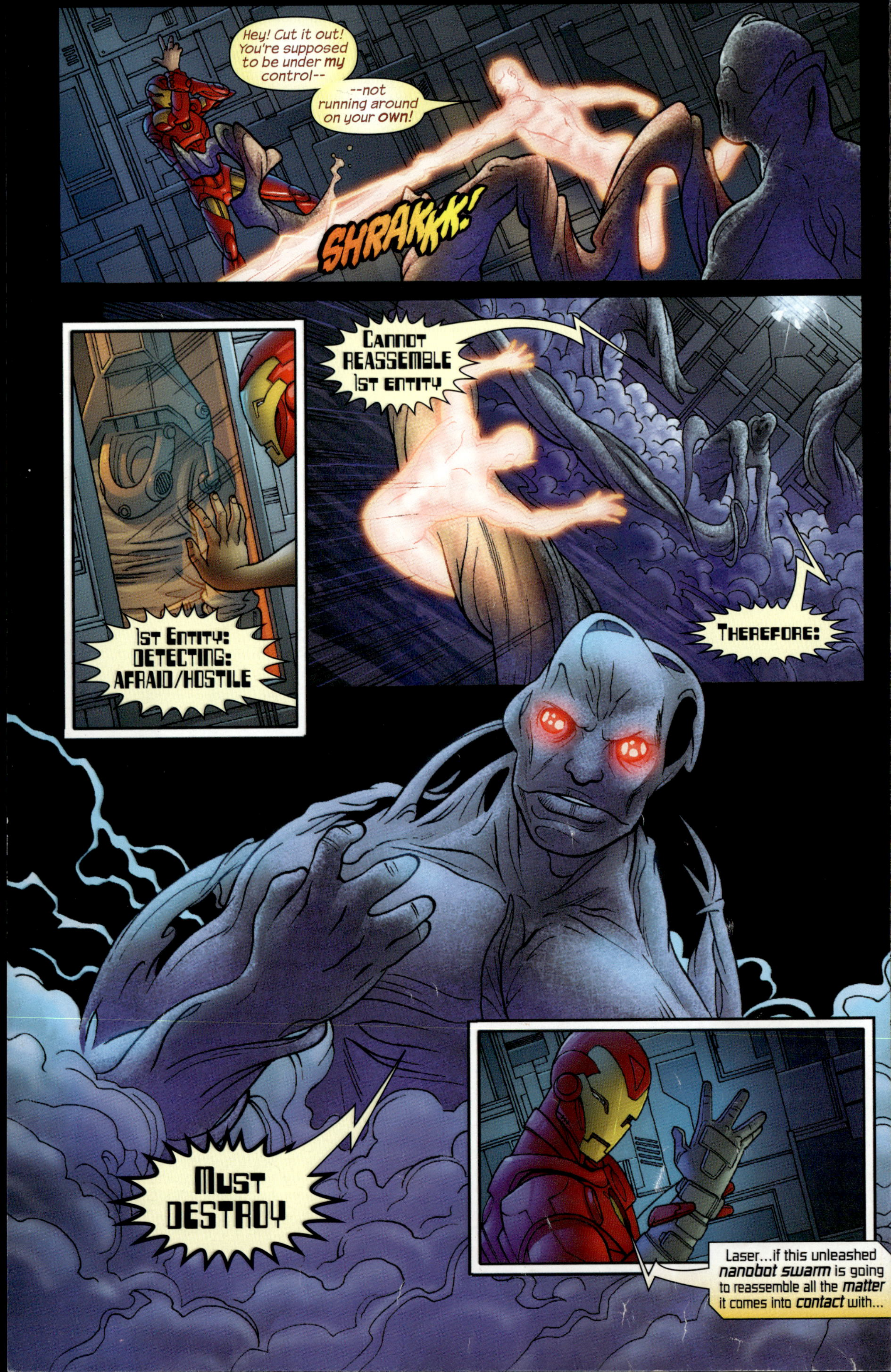
Hey! Cut it out! You're supposed to be under my control--
--not running around on your own!
SHRAKKK!
1st Entity: Detecting: Afraid/Hostile
Cannot reassemble 1st entity
Therefore:
Must destroy
Laser...if this unleashed nanobot swarm is going to reassemble all the matter it comes into contact with...

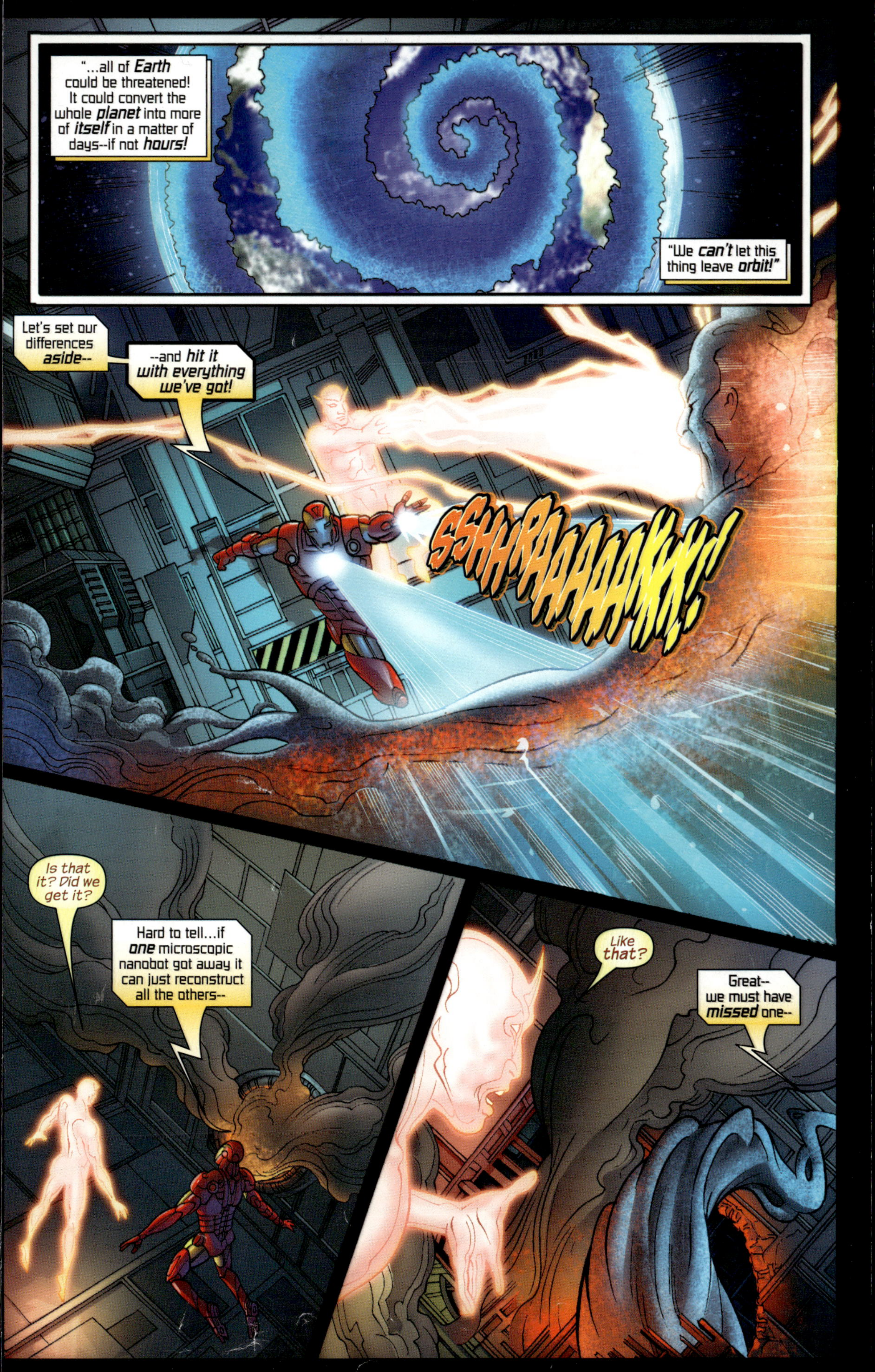
"...all of Earth could be threatened! It could convert the whole planet into more of itself in a matter of days--if not hours!
"We can't let this thing leave orbit!"
Let's set our differences aside--
--and hit it with everything we've got!
SSHHRAAAAAKKK!!
Is that it? Did we get it?
Hard to tell...if one microscopic nanobot got away it can just reconstruct all the others--
Like that?
Great-- we must have missed one--

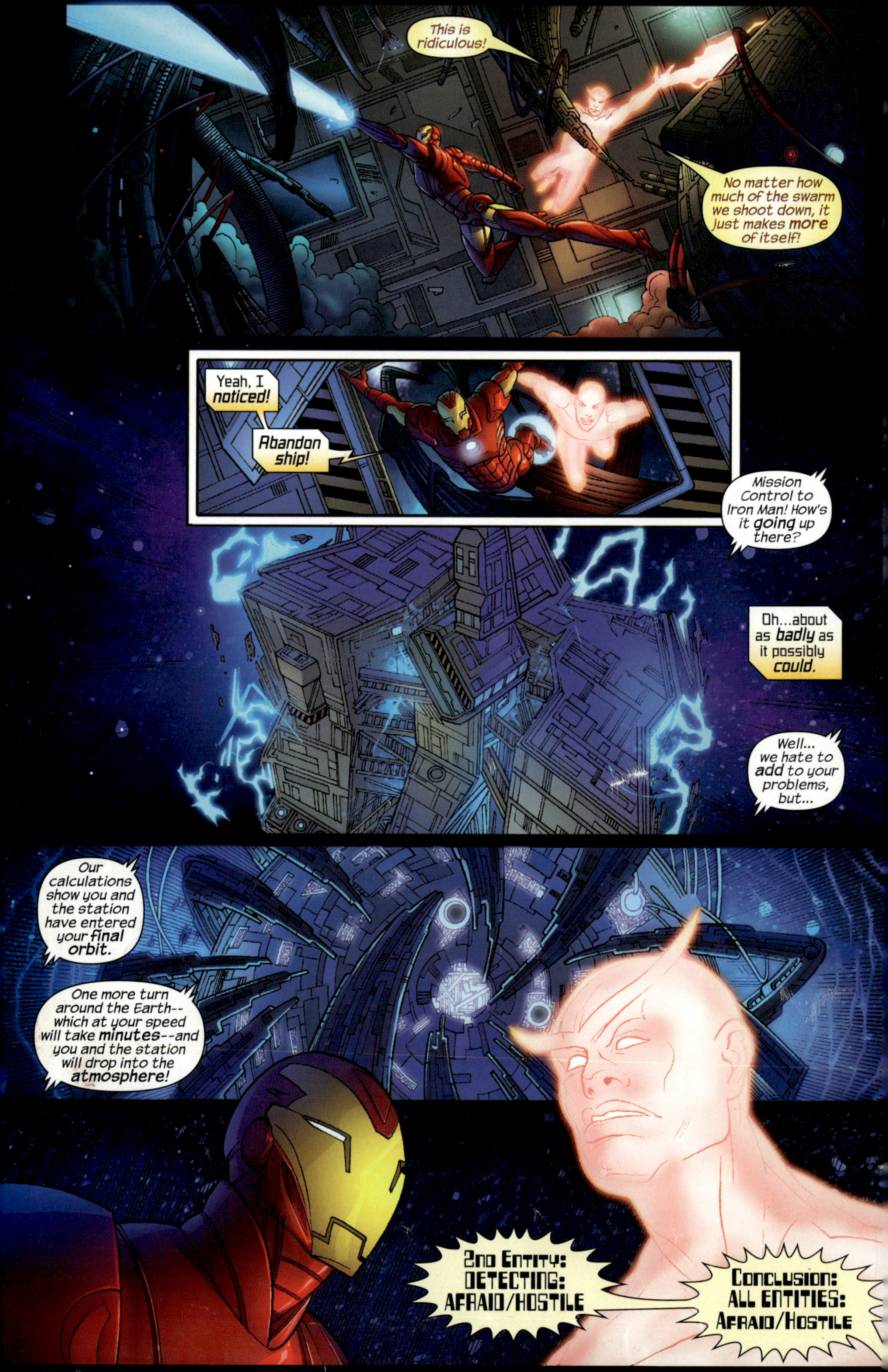

This is ridiculous!
No matter how much of the swarm we shoot down, it just makes more of itself!
Yeah, I noticed!
Abandon ship!
Mission Control to Iron Man! How's it going up there?
Oh...about as badly as it possibly could.
Well... we hate to add to your problems, but...
Our calculations show you and the station have entered your final orbit.
One more turn around the Earth--which at your speed will take minutes--and you and the station will drop into the atmosphere!
2nd Entity: Detecting: Afraid/Hostile
Conclusion: All Entities: Afraid/Hostile

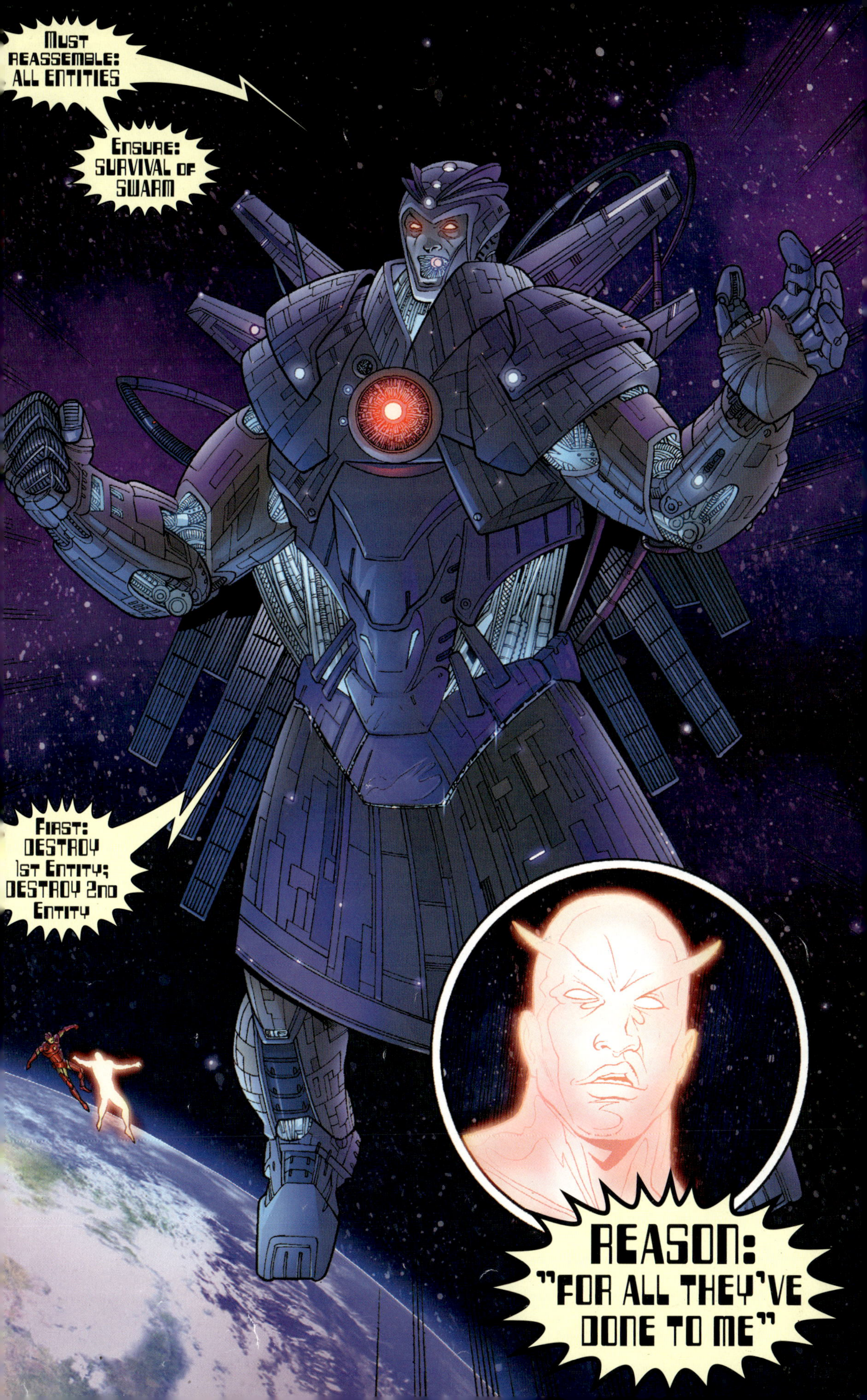
MUST REASSEMBLE: ALL ENTITIES
ENSURE: SURVIVAL OF SWARM
FIRST: DESTROY 1st ENTITY; DESTROY 2nd ENTITY
REASON: "FOR ALL THEY'VE DONE TO ME"

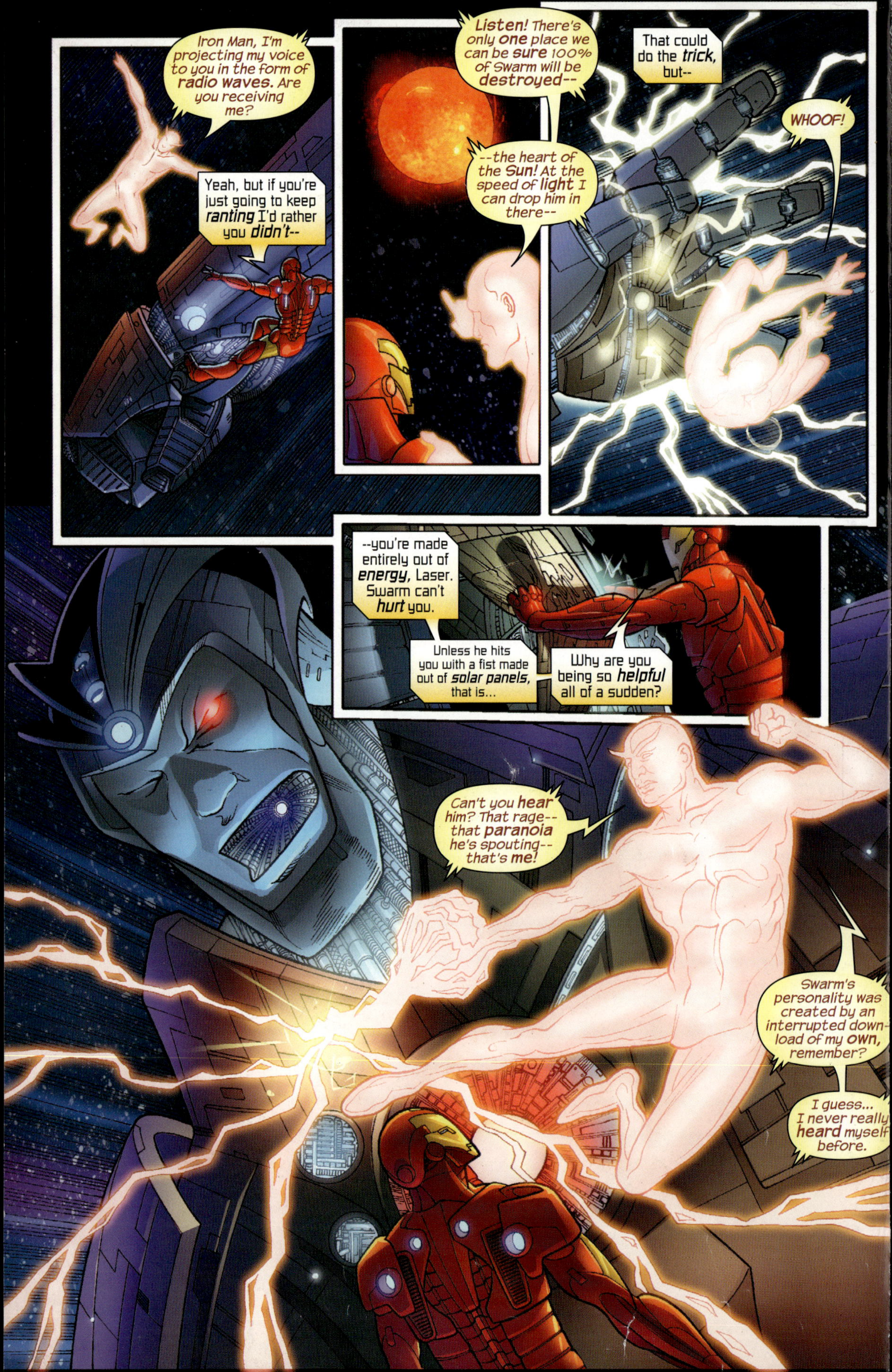
Iron Man, I'm projecting my voice to you in the form of radio waves. Are you receiving me?
Yeah, but if you're just going to keep ranting I'd rather you didn't--
Listen! There's only one place we can be sure 100% of Swarm will be destroyed--
--the heart of the Sun! At the speed of light I can drop him in there--
That could do the trick, but--
WHOOF!
--you're made entirely out of energy, Laser. Swarm can't hurt you.
Unless he hits you with a fist made out of solar panels, that is...
Why are you being so helpful all of a sudden?
Can't you hear him? That rage--that paranoia he's spouting--that's me!
Swarm's personality was created by an interrupted download of my own, remember?
I guess... I never really heard myself before.

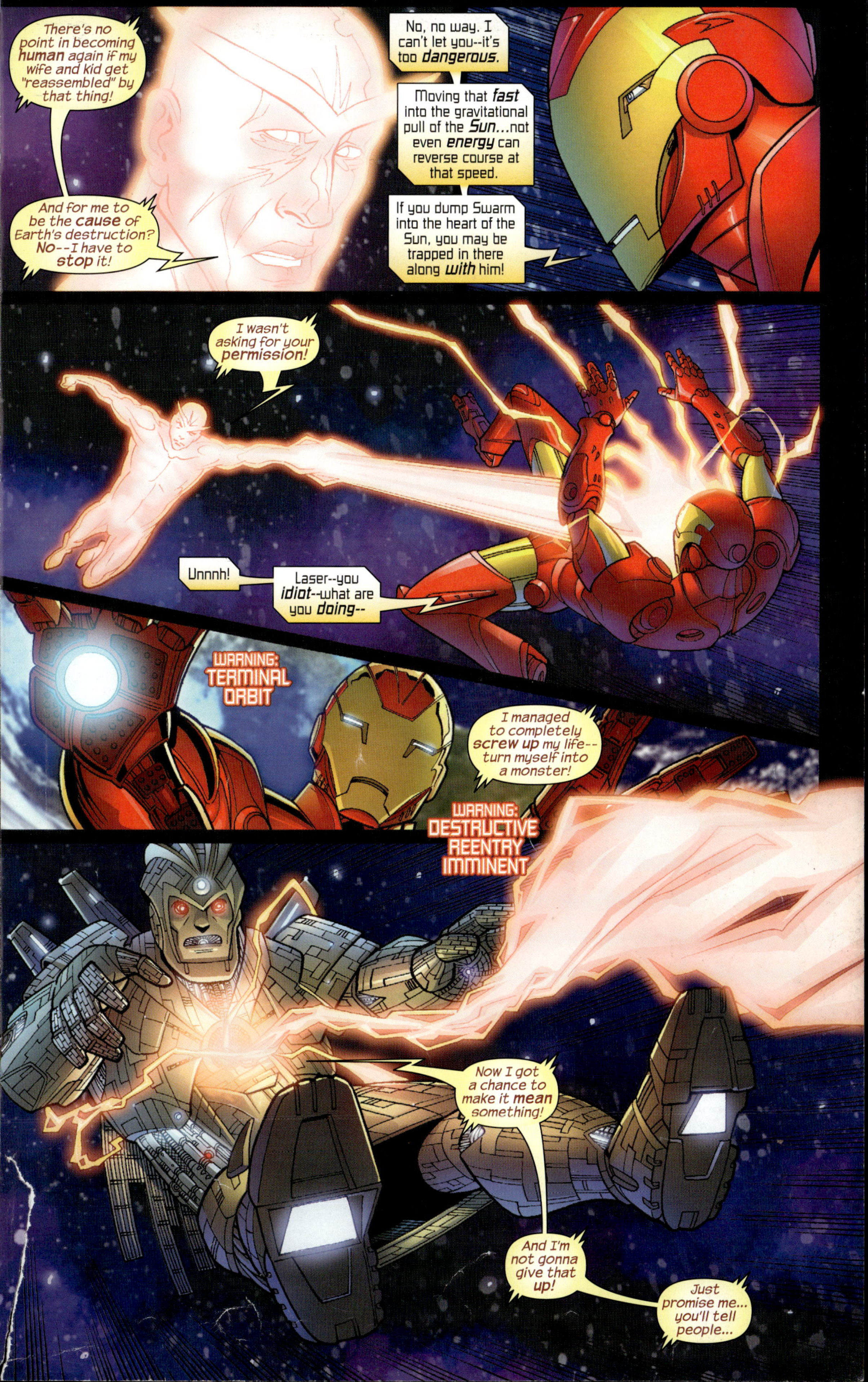

There's no point in becoming human again if my wife and kid get "reassembled" by that thing!
And for me to be the cause of Earth's destruction? No--I have to stop it!
No, no way. I can't let you--it's too dangerous.
Moving that fast into the gravitational pull of the Sun...not even energy can reverse course at that speed.
If you dump Swarm into the heart of the Sun, you may be trapped in there along with him!
I wasn't asking for your permission!
Unnnh!
Laser--you idiot--what are you doing--
WARNING: TERMINAL ORBIT
I managed to completely screw up my life--turn myself into a monster!
WARNING: DESTRUCTIVE REENTRY IMMINENT
Now I got a chance to make it mean something!
And I'm not gonna give that up!
Just promise me... you'll tell people...

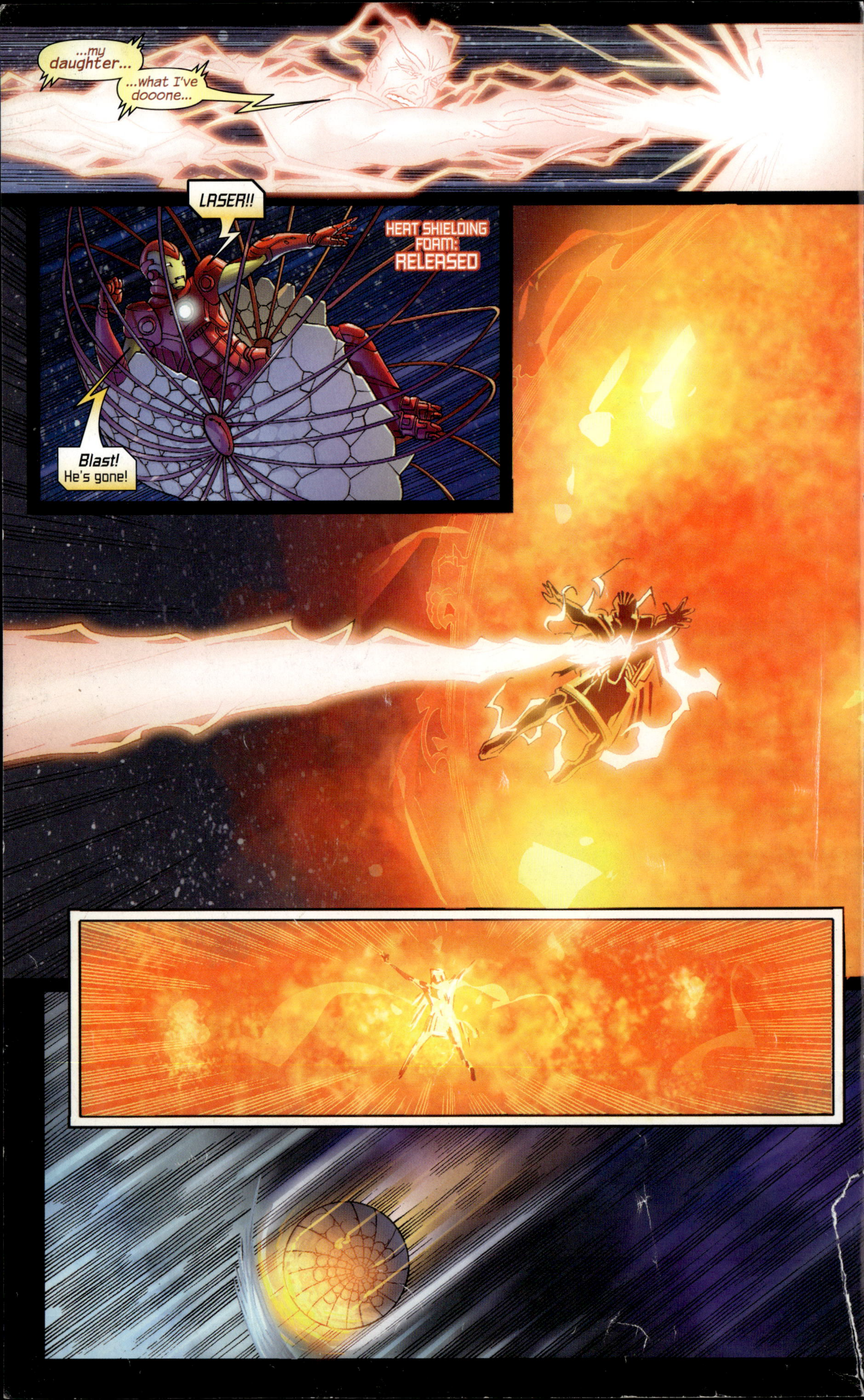
...my daughter...
...what I've dooone...
LASER!!
HEAT SHIELDING FOAM: RELEASED
Blast! He's gone!

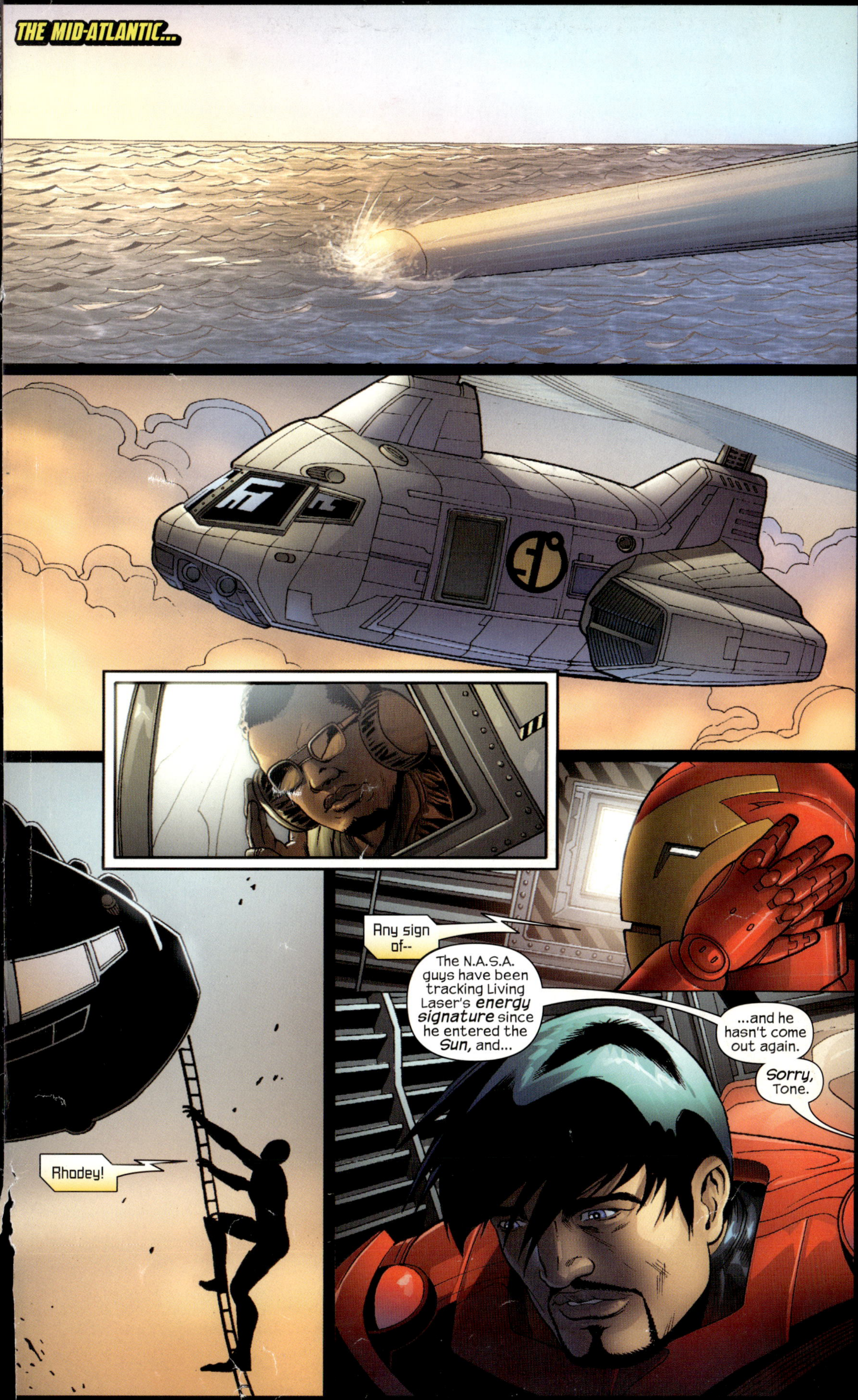
THE MID-ATLANTIC...
Rhodey!
Any sign of--
The N.A.S.A. guys have been tracking Living Laser's energy signature since he entered the Sun, and...
...and he hasn't come out again.
Sorry, Tone.

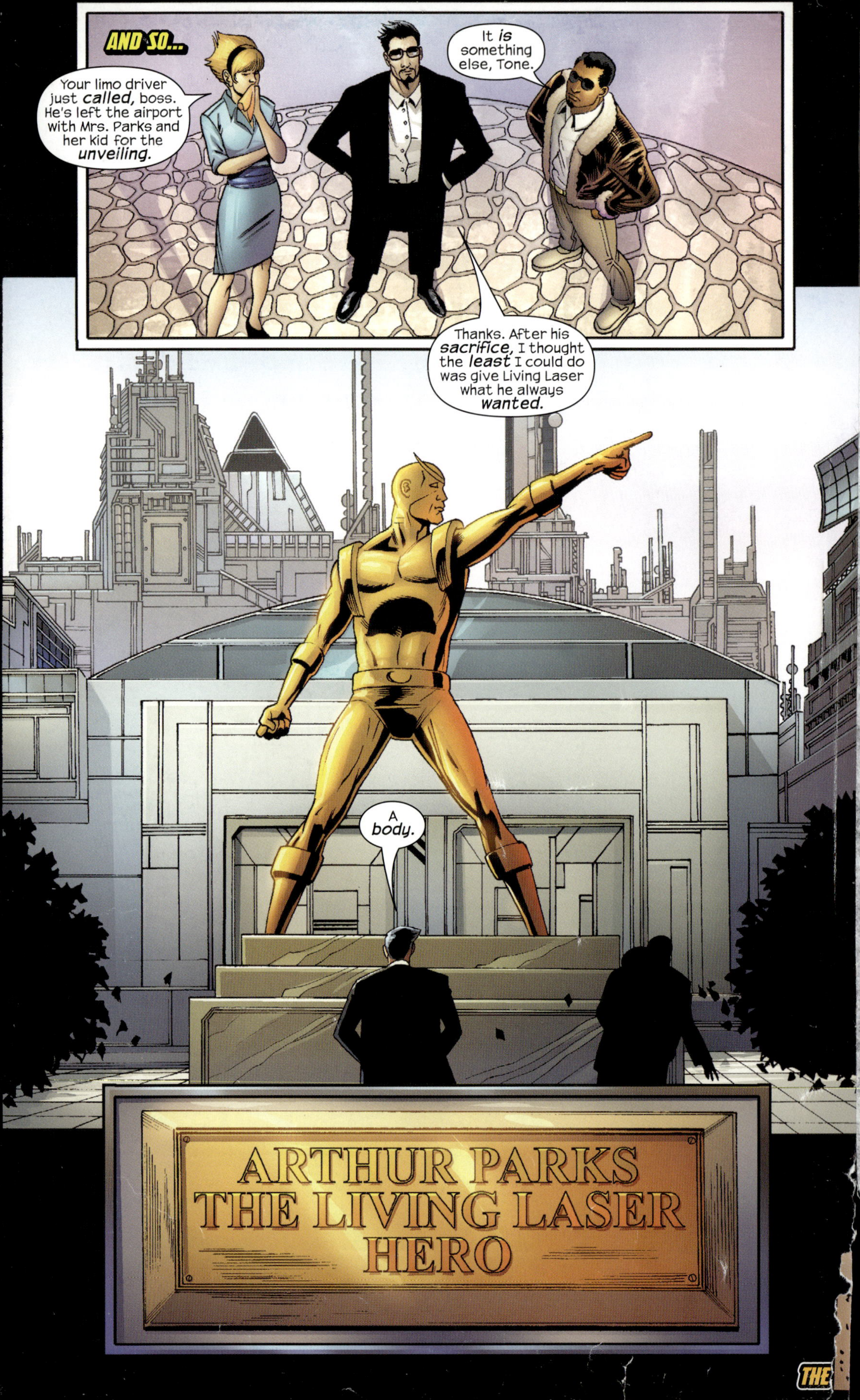
AND SO...
Your limo driver just called, boss. He's left the airport with Mrs. Parks and her kid for the unveiling.
It is something else, Tone.
Thanks. After his sacrifice, I thought the least I could do was give Living Laser what he always wanted.
A body.
ARTHUR PARKS THE LIVING LASER HERO
THE